Gunilla Wolde

THOMAS
has a bath

English text
Alison Winn

HODDER AND STOUGHTON
LONDON SYDNEY AUCKLAND TORONTO

Thomas has a spade,
a rake, a watering can,
and a little red tin
for keeping things in.

He loves sloshing about
with sand and water.

It makes him very dirty
and the only thing to
get him clean again
is *more* water.

So he has a hot splashy bath and a cold tickly shower.

Thomas's grandmother lives
in the country by the sea.
When he stays at her house
she has to put the kettle on
to make hot water for a bath.

Grandmother's bath
is very small.
With Thomas in there,
there isn't much room
for water.

And most of it
seems to get on the floor.

Thomas is sure Grandmother
will be pleased if he mops it up
before he goes to the beach.

The sun is hot and yellow,
and the sea is cool and blue.
"Just the day for a swim,"
says Thomas.

When Thomas has finished
his swim he fills his bucket
with sea water.

And gives Grandmother's flowers a bath.

It begins to rain.
Grandmother's flowers
get two baths.

And Teddy gets sopping wet.

"Funny thing," says Thomas.
"Teddy seems to have got dirtier instead of cleaner."

So Thomas and Teddy
both have a good wash
with clean hot water
and yellow soap.

Just for fun,
Thomas leaps
in the air.

Thomas jumps in the tub.
All the water jumps out.

"Time to clean my teeth now," says Thomas, squeezing out a long wiggly worm of peppermint toothpaste.

Then he brushes his hair.
But the tufty bit on
top just won't lie down.

"Never mind," says Thomas, putting on his blue pyjamas. "Time for bed now."

But Teddy isn't
ready for bed.
He is still sopping
wet and has to
be pegged out
on the line to dry.

"Goodnight, Teddy," calls Thomas.
Then he cuddles down under the bedclothes
and tries to get to sleep quickly.
He is glad it will soon be morning,
so he can slosh about with sand and
water again.